PHILIP PULLMAN

SPRING-HEELED JACK

Illustrated by David Mostyn

PUFFIN

PUFFIN BOOKS

UK | USA | Canada | Ireland | Australia
India | New Zealand | South Africa

Puffin Books is part of the Penguin Random House group of companies
whose addresses can be found at global.penguinrandomhouse.com.

www.penguin.co.uk
www.puffin.co.uk
www.ladybird.co.uk

First published in Great Britain by Doubleday 1989
Published by Corgi Yearling 1991
Published in this edition 2018

001

Text copyright © Philip Pullman, 1989
Illustrations copyright © David Mostyn, 1989

The moral right of the author and illustrator has been asserted

The publisher gratefully acknowledges permission to reprint
extracts from the following publications:
Janet and Allan Ahlberg, *The Jolly Postman, or Other People's Letters*,
William Heinemann Ltd
Shirley Hughes, *It's Too Frightening For Me*, Hodder and Stoughton Ltd
Tove Jansson, *The Exploits of Moominpappa*, Albert Bonniers Forlag
and A & C Black Ltd
Russell Hoban, *The Mouse and His Child*, Faber & Faber
Hergé, *The Adventures of Tintin: The Shooting Star*, Methuen Children's Books

Set in 10/16.5 pt Minister Std Light
Typeset by Jouve (UK), Milton Keynes
Printed in Great Britain by Clays Ltd, St Ives plc

A CIP catalogue record for this book is available from the British Library

ISBN: 978-0- 241-36231-0

All correspondence to:
Puffin Books
Penguin Random House Children's
80 Strand, London WC2R 0RL

For Tom

THE LEGEND OF SPRING-HEELED JACK

IN VICTORIAN times, before Superman and Batman had been heard of, there was another hero who used to go around rescuing people and catching criminals.

This was Spring-Heeled Jack.

No one knew what his real name was; all they knew was that he was dressed like the devil, that he could leap over houses with the help of springs in the heels of his boots, and that any evil-doer who came up against him met a very unpleasant end.

Naturally, a character as mysterious as Spring-Heeled Jack had a lot of stories told about him.

And when people heard that Spring-Heeled Jack had been seen, they stayed indoors and didn't look out of their windows. Because he *might* have been a man, and he might not. And some of his deeds were a little too devilish for comfort . . .

CHAPTER ONE

'It was a dark and stormy night . . .'
Alexandre Dumas, *The Three Musketeers*

IT WAS a dark and stormy night. In the city of London the wind was tossing the boats on the river and driving the rain down every alley, up every flight of steps, and in through every broken window.

No one was out if they had any excuse to stay in. No one respectable, that is. Only alley-cats and criminals had any business in the streets that night, and even they took cover when they could.

High up on the third floor of the Alderman Cawn-Plaster Memorial Orphanage, though, something was stirring.

Rose, Lily, and little Ned had been in the Alderman Cawn-Plaster Memorial Orphanage for eighteen months, ever since their father's ship had sunk in the Indian Ocean. He'd gone to seek his fortune in the goldfields of Australia, and he'd never been heard of since. Their mother had died soon afterwards, and the children had been taken into the Alderman Cawn-Plaster Memorial Orphanage, where the porridge was as thin as the blankets, and as cold as the smiles on the guardians' faces. No wonder they wanted to run away.

The only thing they had to remind them of their mother was a gold locket on a chain. Rose had it still, in spite of the rules of the orphanage, which said that children should give up any jewellery they had to the guardians.

But they'd had enough.

Spangle was quite happy to go with them. There wasn't much love where she came from, and the children had some to spare.

They huddled themselves up against the rain and the wind, and hurried off through the dark streets towards the Docks. At least, they thought they were going towards the Docks, but the streets were so dark, and the night was so foggy, that very soon they hadn't got the faintest idea where they were.

They settled down in the doorway. What a place to sleep! Fog Row was the dirtiest, dankest, miserablest spot in the whole of the East End – and only a spit and a stride from a certain bunch of dustbins.

3

And so they settled down to sleep.

The trouble with that particular bunch of dustbins was this:

This was Mack the Knife, the most evil villain in London, and the dustbin concealed the way in to his secret hideout. There'd never been a more evil man than Mack the Knife. Cats fled, rats fled, policemen fled, murderers fled when Mack arrived. He was the King of Crime.

Oh, the folly of youth, thought Mack the Knife, climbing out from behind the dustbins. How innocent they are! How simple! How lucky I am!

And he bent down low, trying to spot a gleam of gold in the shadows.

All of a sudden Spangle pricked up her ears and smelt him.

'You thief! You villain!' yelled little Ned. 'That locket's going to pay for our escape to America!'

'No, it ain't,' said Mack the Knife. 'It's going to pay for a meat pie and a bottle of brandy. Now hand it over.'

'Never!' cried Ned.

And he and Spangle threw themselves at Mack the Knife, punching and kicking and snarling and biting and spitting, and it did them no good at all.

But with Rose to one side and Lily to the other, and not knowing which of them had the locket, Mack the Knife was foxed. If he went after Lily, and Rose had it, he'd get nothing; but if Lily had it, and he went after Rose, he'd still get nothing.

On the other hand, he had Ned already.

They just didn't know what to do. 'Don't give it to him, sisters!' cried Ned. 'Be indomitable!'

'Such language,' said Mack. 'Well, I tell you what. You bring that locket here by daybreak, and you can have your little brother back in one piece. If you don't, you can have him back in lots of pieces. It's up to you.'

'But – but –'

'Come along, cully!'

And off he went, sneaking away into the shadows with Ned folded up under his arm.

A pitiful state of affairs!

Just then, a troubling rumble of thunder trundled across the sky. The wisps of fog were whisked aside, and the girls looked up at the stars and saw –

HELP!

The devil?

Well, if he wasn't the devil, then who the devil was he?

Then the figure sprang through the air like a firework, and landed –

Right in front of the girls.
Who **SCREAMED**!

Spring-Heeled Jack blinked. It was as if someone today said, 'Who's Batman?'

Rose and Lily followed as Spring-Heeled Jack led them through a maze of narrow alleys, past crumbling warehouses and sordid opium dens, and on the way told him their story.

When they'd finished, Spring-Heeled Jack scowled with anger.

'I'll stop at nothing!' he said. 'Your little brother will be restored, and you shall have your tickets to America. I know a safe retreat where you can stay. Fear not, for Spring-Heeled Jack is on the way . . .'

And off they went, at top speed, through the back streets and the squares and the alleyways, towards a certain pub in Blackfriars.

CHAPTER TWO

'Meanwhile, back at the ranch . . .' *A Western*

MEANWHILE, BACK at the orphanage, the Superintendent's assistant had made a horrid discovery.

'Mr Killjoy!' she said, bursting into the office, where the Superintendent was doing the accounts. He often did them late at night, to avoid being overlooked.

'What? What? What?' he said, hiding the brandy.

She told him.

'Item: Rose Summers. Item: Lily Summers. Item: Ned Summers,' she said. 'Condition: missing, together with one institutional blanket, one loaf of institutional bread (last week's quality), and one item of personal property, to wit, a forbidden locket and chain.'

He gaped in horror.

'And when was this discovered?' he said.

'At half-past eight,' said Miss Gasket, 'when I was a-going on my rounds, as laid down in my conditions of service. All the beds I looked in, every blessed one, was full of kids, and all asleep, as per the rules, in the regulation posture, hands by sides and eyes shut. All but three, that is. And there was a window open.'

'Do my ears deceive me?' said Mr Killjoy. 'We'll have to get 'em back at once. Ooh, they'll cop it when I gets hold of 'em. Think of Clause 44, Miss Gasket! Think of that, and shiver!'

She did.

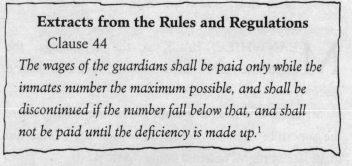

Extracts from the Rules and Regulations
Clause 44

The wages of the guardians shall be paid only while the inmates number the maximum possible, and shall be discontinued if the number fall below that, and shall not be paid until the deficiency is made up.[1]

1. In other words, if they didn't cram in as many kids as the place would hold, they didn't get any wages.

Mr Killjoy's mighty brain was starting to hum.

'We'll go straight to my friend Sergeant Pincher at the Hangman's Wharf Police Station,' he said. 'We'll have all the minions of the law combing London for the little perishers. Besides . . .'

Mr Killjoy locked the accounts away, just in case anyone should come across them by chance and fail to understand them, and then he and his assistant put on their coats and hats and went out to see Sergeant Pincher.

CHAPTER THREE

'What happened next
We'll very soon see . . .'
Janet and Allan Ahlberg, *The Jolly Postman,
or Other People's Letters*

WHAT HAPPENED next took place on board the good ship *Indomitable*. She was snug in dock, and all kinds of nautical activity were taking place. Sailors were belaying the taffrail to the bowsprit, boxing the compass, and splicing the binnacle. There was a lot to do before the ship sailed in the morning.

Captain Webster was sitting up in the bridge looking at charts, when Jim Bowling, an Able Seaman, came up and saluted.

'Gentleman to see you, sir,' he said. 'A Mr Summers.'

'Summers,' said the Captain. 'I know that name . . . Well, show him up, show him up!'

The Captain stowed the charts and turned to face his visitor. And then he remembered Mr Summers, who'd been a passenger on his ship some time before.

19

They sat down together and called for grog. 'The last time we met,' said the Captain, 'you were coming to England on business, if I remember.'

'That's right,' said Mr Summers. 'It seems a long time ago now. Remarkably fine grog, Andrew.'

Mr Summers' Story

Seven years before, he had gone off to seek his fortune in the Australian goldfields (what an extraordinary coincidence!), and when his ship had sunk, he'd been captured by pirates and forced to toil at an oar with chains around his ankles. When at last he managed to escape, he struggled to raise the cash to come back to England and search for his dear wife and his three little children – Rose, and Lily, and Ned.

21

'No,' said Mr Summers, 'I've searched high and low in every part of the country, and found . . . nothing. I can stay in England no longer. I must go abroad, and start a new life in a distant country. Have you room for a passenger?'

'My dear old chap!' said the Captain. 'There's always room for you. But you're just in time – we sail with the morning tide.'

Jim Bowling saluted smartly and left. The Captain showed Mr Summers to a comfortable cabin, and the sailors went on reefing the foremast, furling the capstan, and holystoning the futtock shrouds. It was a busy ship.

HOW TO HOLYSTONE A FUTTOCK SHROUD

(A) TAKE THE BIGHT OF THE STANDING PART AND BEND IT TO THE LUFF.

(C) FURL THE KEDGE TO THE FLUKES AND BELAY THE SHANK TO THE TURK'S HEAD.

(B) UNHOIST THE REEFING PENDANT ON THE STARBOARD CRINGLE AND BELAY IT TO THE GAFF.

(D) REEVE THE LUFF TACKLE THROUGH THE JIB HALYARDS AND MAKE IT FAST WITH A FISHERMAN'S FRIEND.

(E) TAKE A LUMP OF HOLYSTONE AND SCRUB THE DECK.

?

I SHOULD HAVE STAYED AT HOME

CHAPTER FOUR

'It was a gloomy old place with high brick walls . . .'
Shirley Hughes, *It's Too Frightening For Me*

IN THE murkiest, slimiest, darkest corner of the East End, there was a crumbling old warehouse that even the rats had deserted. One side of it leaned crazily out over the river, and the other side leaned gloomily out over the street.

It was called TURNER AND LUCKETT'S MEDICINAL SARSAPARILLA WAREHOUSE but there'd been no sarsaparilla stored there for years. People believed it was haunted. Mysterious lights used to gleam behind the broken windows high up on the top floor, and hideous noises came filtering out over the rooftops in the middle of the night.

It was the headquarters of Mack the Knife and his appalling gang.

When he reached the warehouse, with little Ned still struggling under his arm, Mack went straight to the top floor, where a bunch of gangsters were sitting around a table playing cards by the light of a stolen candle.

Their names were Quinlan, Peregrine, Auberon, and Filthy.

QUINLAN   PEREGRINE   MACK   AUBERON   FILTHY

YOU OUGHT TO SELL THEIR FACES TO A CHEESECAKE FACTORY, TO CURDLE THE MILK. YOU OUGHT TO SELL THEIR FACES TO POSTMEN, TO FRIGHTEN DOGS WITH.

YOU OUGHT TO SELL THEIR FACES TO A TEMPERANCE SOCIETY, TO DISPLAY AS AN EVIL VISION BROUGHT ON BY DRINK!

The gang hadn't met a cheeky victim before, and they didn't like it. They'd have been very nasty indeed to Ned if Mack hadn't stopped them.

'Get back!' he said, beating them off. 'The little feller's right, you're the ugliest bunch I've ever seen. Come on, where's that rope?'

Filthy handed him a length of rope. Mack took out his knife to cut through a knot in it.

'Here, go steady, boss,' said Filthy. 'That rope's got sentimental value for me. They hanged my Uncle Charlie with it last week.'

'More fool him for getting caught,' said Mack.

'Now hold him still while I truss him up.'

YOU GREAT BULLIES! YOU UGLY SO-AND-SO'S! YOU GREEDY MURDERING SAUSAGE-FACED PUDDING-HEADED IDLE CONNIVING SCOUNDRELS! YOU FAT-BELLIED STONY-HEARTED SHARK-FACED TIGHT-FISTED SONS OF CRIME! YOU WON'T GET ANYTHING OUT OF THIS, 'CAUSE I'M INDOMITABLE!

'Hark at him, Filthy, what eloquence!' said Mack, when they'd finally got him tied up. 'If you ever get out of this, son, take my advice: become a lawyer. It's the same as thieving, only respectable, and there's no risk of getting caught.'

Ned blew a raspberry that shook the window-frames.

'Dear, dear, dear,' said Peregrine. 'Can't have that. Shall I snite his snitch?'[1]

'Shall I mill his rattlers?'[2] said Auberon.

'Shall I nob him on the canister?'[3] said Quinlan.

'No, no, no,' said Mack the Knife. 'You know your trouble, boys? You got no craft. You got no imagination. This little feller's going to make us a lot of money. Quinlan, go and steal me some fish and chips. And a bottle of brandy while you're about it.'

1. Snite his snitch: give him a good flap in the face.
2. Mill his rattlers: knock his teeth out.
3. Nob him on the canister: whack him on the head.

Now all that time, little Spangle had been faithfully following Ned's scent. It wasn't easy for her, because she was only short, and Mack the Knife had carried Ned in the air for a long way; but finally she reached the sarsaparilla warehouse and squeezed her way through a hole in the wall.

Up the dark stairs she trotted, all in the dark, until she reached the room where the gangsters were tying Ned up.

The moment she saw what they were up to, she sprang in fearlessly.

But it was no use. Brave as she was, she just wasn't big enough, and although she managed to nip them all, they very soon had her under control.

'Tut, tut,' said Mack. 'I can't abide all these harsh feelings. I'm going next door to play me violin. Sling him in the corner – where the spiders are.'

So poor Ned was put in the darkest, spideriest corner of the warehouse, and soon the air was filled with hideous howls and screeching sounds, as Mack played hymns on his violin.

The gang put their earplugs in, and went back to their game of cards.

CHAPTER FIVE

'Underneath the arches . . .'
Flanagan and Allen

UNDERNEATH THE arches near Blackfriars Bridge, a lonely pieman was wheeling his hot-pie-wagon along, and whistling to keep his spirits up. There was hardly anyone about that night; he hadn't sold a pie for over an hour.

Then he heard a familiar tune. It was *Santa Lucia*, played on the barrel-organ of his friend Antonio Rolipolio.

He turned the corner and saw the organ-grinder outside the Rose and Crown, with his monkey Miranda capering about on the barrel-organ. But there was no one listening to him. The streets were deserted.

'Poor folks like us have got to take our chance,' said the pieman. 'Hot pies! Hot pies!'

'Funiculi, funicula,' agreed the organ-grinder.

Just then, who should come round the corner but the sailor from the *Indomitable*, Able-Seaman Jim Bowling. He was glad to be out and about, in spite of the cold, because it gave him the chance to come and say farewell yet again to his sweetheart, Polly Pickles, the barmaid at the Rose and Crown.

He went inside and fetched her out, and they stood beneath the gaslight on the corner of the street to say a tender goodbye.

'Oh, Jim, my beloved, farewell!' she said.

'Farewell, Polly!' he said. 'We're off to Baltimore and Panama, and Trebizond and Trinidad and Trincomalee, and Auckland and Shanghai and Wagga Wagga, and it'll be years before I'm back in London. Don't forget me, Polly!'

But it was no good asking Jim to buy anything. His pockets were empty.

'I reckon we're all in the same fix, mates,' he said. 'Still, Polly, I'll pick up a shilling or two tonight, 'cause there's a gent on board who wants his case picked up before we sail. I dare say he'll slip me a bit of money, if I gets it to him smartish. So I'm off now, Polly, love, and the first stop on the way to Baltimore is the Saveloy Hotel!'

'Oh, sweetheart!' said Polly. 'Take care!'

'I will!'

'And come back safe!'

'I will!'

'And don't forget your little Polly!'

'As if I ever could!'

The pieman and the organ-grinder, not to mention the monkey, were overcome at the sight of such devotion.

And so Jim left, leaving Polly weeping under the gaslight.

'Well, there's no money for us here, mate,' said the pieman. 'Time to move on. Hot pies! Hot pies!'

And he trundled his pie-wagon away. The organ-grinder sat his monkey back on the organ and began to pack up too.

'Come along, monkey,' he said. 'Good-a night, pretty Polly. Love will-a find a way!'

'Good night, Signor Rolipolio,' said Polly. 'Good night, monkey . . .'

Oh, well, thought Polly. Some day my Jim will come back, and then we'll be as happy as fleas on a nice warm dog.

She was just about to go back into the pub when –

Polly knew Spring-Heeled Jack well. He'd saved her from some robbers only a month or two before, so she wasn't afraid of him at all. And when she heard what he had to say, she was glad to help.

'Ooh, that's awful!' she said, when they told her about Mack the Knife and Ned and the locket and everything. 'But you come inside – you'll be safe here. You can rely on Jack. If anyone can save your little brother, he can!'

And he leapt away over the rooftops with incredible speed, making a whizzing noise like a firework and leaving a trail of smoke in the air.

'Oh, miss,' said Rose, 'we're in such trouble!'

'We must get Ned back, you see,' said Lily, 'and then get to the Docks in time, and . . .'

'There, there,' said Polly. 'You come on in. I'll see if I can find you a sandwich. You look as if you could do with a feed.'

So in they went, and the cold, foggy street was empty again.

But not for long.

Because an odd bedraggled little creature like a mournful moth, or like a second-hand angel, was flapping dismally through the foggy air, invisible to everyone except us. It flew in and hovered near the window of the pub, as if it was waiting for someone.

And a second later, that someone arrived. It was Filthy.

Filthy was ambitious. Besides, he didn't much like what Mack the Knife was up to. He thought there'd be openings for a smart young man, and he'd spotted something going on a minute ago outside the Rose and Crown – something he could turn to his advantage.

So he crept up to the window – and the little shabby moth-like thing came and sat on his shoulder.

That was how they dealt with consciences in London. The other members of the gang had no consciences at all, or else they'd got rid of them better than Filthy had. With an uneasy look behind him, Filthy went into the Rose and Crown.

CHAPTER SIX

'There is an air of cold, solitary desolation
about the noiseless streets . . .'
Charles Dickens, *Sketches by Boz*

THERE WAS an air of cold, solitary desolation about
the noiseless streets. Mr Killjoy and Miss Gasket
had been combing them for hours, and Sergeant Pincher
from the Hangman's Wharf Police Station had got his
best men searching too. There was hardly a corner of
London they didn't poke their noses into. They were only
bothering because of the locket, of course.

And not long after Rose and Lily arrived at the Rose
and Crown, and only a minute or two after Filthy did, Mr
Killjoy and Miss Gasket did too.

They were feeling chilly, and Mr Killjoy was thinking
that he'd like to slip into the saloon bar for a large brandy.
It wouldn't be fitting for a lady to be seen in a public
house, so he'd send out a glass of lemonade for Miss
Gasket while she kept watch on the pavement.

He was just explaining this to her when he felt a tap on
his shoulder.

Filthy looked around nervously in case his conscience was watching, but he couldn't see it, so he went on:

'I thought as how I heard the lady here address you as Mr Killjoy, and I thought to myself, I thought, I wonder if this could be the Mr Albert Killjoy as runs the Alderman Cawn-Plaster Memorial Orphanage?'

'That person has the honour of being me,' said Mr Killjoy austerely. 'Well, my man, what is it? What is it?'

'Get off,' muttered Filthy, brushing something off his shoulder. 'I beg your pardon, sir. The thing is – I knows the whereabouts of a certain pair of little girls.'

'Oh,' said Mr Killjoy. 'Ah.'

Then Miss Gasket took him aside.

Mr Killjoy was a soft touch, but Miss Gasket was terrifying. Filthy nearly quailed as she glared at him.

'I suppose you intend to ask a price for this information?' she said.

'Well,' said Filthy, 'I thought maybe a payment of five guineas would cover it. Sort of an honorarium, kind of thing.'

'A dishonorarium, more like,' said Miss Gasket. 'I'll give you *one*, and that's your lot.'

Mr Killjoy was deeply impressed, but Filthy wasn't.

'One guinea?' he said, shocked. 'One guinea, after all I've done? If you said four, now . . .'

'If I agreed to four, I'd be a fool,' said Miss Gasket. 'Two at the most.'

'Make it three?' said Filthy humbly.

'Certainly not,' she said. 'Two, and that's your lot.'

Mr Killjoy handed Filthy two guineas. Filthy stowed them inside his pocket quickly before his conscience saw how much he'd got.

So Filthy slunk away. But around the corner –

OH NO! NOT YOU AGAIN! I SHALL HAVE A ROTTEN NIGHT, AND NO MISTAKE...

Inside the Rose and Crown, Mr Killjoy was demanding to see Polly Pickles.

'She's in the public bar,' said the landlord, 'doing her job, what she's paid for. She's spent enough time this evening canoodling with her sweetheart.'

'Don't argue with me,' said Mr Killjoy. 'Have you a private parlour, my man?'

'Yes, I have, and it costs a guinea to hire it,' said the landlord. Mr Killjoy drew himself up to his full height, and then handed over a guinea.

'Be good enough to show us in there,' he said. 'And subsequently have this Pickles person brought before us, or else face the full rigour of the law.'

The landlord said something rude, which Miss Gasket didn't quite catch, and then went to fetch Polly.

'We'll have to play this careful,' said Mr Killjoy to Miss Gasket as they went into the parlour. 'We don't want 'em to take fright and skedaddle.'

So when Polly came in a minute later, they were all smiles and sweetness.

'Now, Miss Pickles,' said Miss Gasket, 'three of our little charges has gone astray. Our *dear* little charges. And naturally we're upset and concerned –'

'And we've come searching for them,' said Mr Killjoy, 'sparing no expense of time or money –'

'Just so's we get our little darlings back!' said Miss Gasket.

'Well, I don't know,' said Polly. 'They did say they came from the Alderman Cawn-Plaster Memorial Orphanage, not the Happy Smiles whatever-it-was . . .'

'The little monkeys!' said Mr Killjoy, fondly. 'Always ready for a joke, them kids. We've laughed together many a time, haven't we, Miss Gasket?'

'Oh, those jolly evenings in the Home,' she said, 'with the little darlings around our feet, playing their merry tricks!'

Polly wasn't used to dealing with important people, and these two seemed very important. And she wasn't used to dealing with crafty deceptive sneaks either. These two were worse than weasels, but she didn't know they were lying.

43

'Well,' she said, 'I'm not sure . . .'

'There,' said Miss Gasket. 'You're anxious about their safety, I can tell.'

'Yes, I am,' said Polly. 'They're ever so upset, the pair of them, and worn out too.'

'Ahh,' said Miss Gasket fondly.

'You fetch 'em here, Miss Pickles,' said Mr Killjoy. 'Take it from me, they'll be overjoyed to come home again. They'll be frantic with glee.'

'Well, if you say so, sir,' said Polly, 'I'll have to believe you, you being in your position and me being in mine, and the world being what it is. All right, I'll fetch 'em out.'

And out she went, and a short while later she came back with the girls.

And before they could get away, Mr Killjoy had seized Lily in his great red hands. But Rose was too quick for Miss Gasket; she dodged out of the room and down the corridor as quick as a cat.

'Stop! Stop, you hussy!' cried Miss Gasket. 'Come back here!'

'Run, Rose, quick!' shouted Polly. 'Go to the Saveloy Hotel – ask for Jim Bowling! He'll help you!'

And Rose was gone.

Without another word, Mr Killjoy and Miss Gasket swept out, dragging poor Lily behind them.

'Oh, Lily, I'm sorry!' Polly cried, and she tried to hold on to Lily's hand, but they were too strong for her. She ran to the door after them, only to see them disappear around the corner, with Lily still calling Mr Killjoy every name Polly had ever heard of, and several she hadn't.

'Oh, what a fool I am!' she said to herself. 'How could I let meself be taken in like that? Them poor kids, and they was relying on me, and I handed 'em over just like that . . .'

Poor Polly. It wasn't her fault, but she felt it was, and that was bad enough. Saying goodbye to Jim, and then this . . . It was too much. She howled and howled.

And meanwhile Rose was running full tilt through the dark streets, looking for the Saveloy Hotel . . .

CHAPTER SEVEN

'I didn't dare stop to rest . . .'

Tove Jansson, *The Exploits of Moominpappa*

ROSE DIDN'T dare stop to rest. She ran like the wind, up alleyways, across busy squares, down desolate streets. She couldn't afford to be afraid of what might be hiding around dark corners. From the Rose and Crown she ran full tilt until she came to the Strand, and then she stopped and looked up and down.

The gaslights shone down on hansom cabs and carriages, on gentlemen in top hats and flower-girls in rags. There were theatres and restaurants and embassies and clubs, and the biggest, poshest, swankiest place of all was the Saveloy Hotel.

SAVELOY HOTEL
MENU

Le clear soup
Le thick soup
Le soup avec bits in
Le soup de turtle

Le fish avec beaucoup de bones
Le fish avec no bones
Le sauce pour le fish
Le waiter pour le sauce over le fish

Le roast boeuf
La vache entière en croûte à la Desperate Dan[1]
Le roast mouton avec le sauce de mint
Les saucissons dans une montagne de pommes de terre mashés
Le suprême de volaille à la rencontre du King of Brazil avec
sa Petite Amie du Moment

Les végétables
Les chips
Les beans bakés

Le green salade
Le salade de tous les autres couleurs

Le dick spotté
Le jelly
Le blancmange
L'ice cream
Les pancakes

Les sardines sur toast
Les eggs scramblés

Le coffee
Le brandy
Les cigars
Le Turkish Delight

* Cow pie.

CHIEF - BOWER -
AND - SCRAPER

RECEPTION - DESK -
POINTER - OUTER

STAIRCASE - POINTER
OUTER - AND - PORTER -
SUMMONER

When Rose got to the hotel entrance, and looked in at all those servants and guests, her heart sank. How was she going to get past all that poshness, dressed in rags as she was?

However, there was always the back door. She might be able to get in and find Jim Bowling that way. The trouble was, she didn't even know who Jim Bowling was, or what he looked like, or anything. Still, he was her only hope, so she slipped down the courtyard beside the hotel and looked for the back way in.

Meanwhile, in the great kitchen, twenty sauce cooks and thirty meat cooks and forty vegetable cooks and fifty pastry cooks were preparing a banquet for the King of Brazil and all the other guests. The chief cook was shouting at them all, and the cooks were shouting at the waiters, and the waiters were shouting at each other, and the air was full of delicious smells and ferocious heat.

PAGEBOY - CALLER - AND - SENDER - ON - ERRANDS

PORTER

PAGEBOY (WATCH OUT FOR HIM IN A PAGE OR TWO)

In the middle of all the noise and rush, Jim Bowling was making his way out with Mr Summers' suitcase. Since he was only a common sailor, they couldn't possibly let him go out through the front door. But Jim didn't mind, because he suddenly spotted an old friend.

'Casey Wilkins!' he said. 'Shiver me timbers and blow me down, but wherever I go, Shanghai or San Francisco or Bombay, I'm sure to find some old shipmate ashore, snug in a cushy berth and good for a glass of grog. How are you, Casey?'

Casey Wilkins was long, lean, and miserable. He'd been a ship's carpenter when Jim had sailed with him. He was a pastrycook now, and he was kneading some pastry for some *viande de saucisses en croute a la graisse froide*.[1]

'Hello, Jim,' he said. 'Keep your voice down. See that fat cook? The bloke in charge? He's worse than any bosun you've ever sailed with, mate. Wherever you go, there's blokes whose only job is bossing the likes of you and me around.'

1. Sausage rolls.

'Still the same old cheerful spirit,' said Jim.

'What's the rush for? Is it extra busy tonight?'

'We've got the King of Brazil in,' said Casey. 'He likes his food, King Alfonso does.'

'Oh, the King of Brazil, eh,' said Jim. 'Posh.' The fat cook came past with a saucepan, and Jim couldn't resist.

At that moment the door at the far end of the kitchen opened and Rose looked through. No one noticed her in all the hubbub, but she spotted Jim at once, because he was the only person in the place not dressed like a cook.

And Rose was just about to do that when someone else ran up. This time it was a pageboy. The place was definitely getting crowded.

It's all kicks and no ha'pence, being a pageboy.

Casey Wilkins led Jim and Rose up the servants' staircase and along lots of narrow corridors and then up some more stairs into an attic.

'What do we do?' said Jim, who was getting nervous already.

'Nothing to it,' said Casey. 'Just squeeze out through the skylight and there you are, mate. It's a bit steep and slippery, mind – just hang on to the chimneys and you'll be all right . . .'

He had to leave them then and go back and make some more pastry.

53

Jim squeezed out first with the suitcase and Rose came after him, listening carefully all the time for Miss Gasket and the policeman. They wobbled their way along the roof, clinging tightly to the chimneys. Rose had to tell Jim where to put his feet, because he had his eyes shut.

Meanwhile, Miss Gasket had gone through all the rooms in the hotel like a simoom.[1] The policeman trailed nervously behind her, apologizing. He was called P.C. Tweedle. He wasn't much good at chasing people; what he liked best was helping them across the road. He'd never met anyone as fierce as Miss Gasket before, and he wasn't sure how fierce she wanted him to be.

'Er – excuse me, miss –' he said, as she came charging out of a linen cupboard like a khamsin.[2]

'No, they're not in there,' she said. 'Come on. We'll do the attics next. Wake up, man! Move yourself!'

And off she went like a harmattan.[3] Gulping, he followed her up the stairs.

1. A hot wind.
2. A hot wind.
3. A hot wind.

54

Of course, they found nothing in the attics except beetles and woodworms, and it wasn't long before Miss Gasket saw the skylight. It was still open, because Rose hadn't managed to shut it from outside, and Jim couldn't have shut it anyway with his eyes closed.

With a snort of derision, Miss Gasket told P.C. Tweedle to kneel down. She stood on his shoulders and hauled herself through the skylight, and then pulled him up after her. He didn't like it at all.

And at the other end of the roof . . .

55

P.C. Tweedle was horrified. He didn't like heights any more than Jim did.

'He looks dangerous to me,' he said. 'He's a desperate character, miss. He's probably got knives and guns and dynamite in that suitcase. I think we'd better call for reinforcements –'

Miss Gasket hit him.

'Ow!' he said. 'All right, all right – I'll arrest him.'

'He says he ain't, miss,' said P.C. Tweedle. 'Perhaps we'd better –'

Then he saw the look in Miss Gasket's eye, and ducked. Her handbag went whistling past his head.

'You're a lily-livered poltroon,' she told him. 'You're a disgrace to your noble helmet. I'll have to go and get him myself!'

Jim certainly didn't want to fall off, but he certainly didn't want any more of Miss Gasket.

'Hang on there, Rose,' he shouted. 'I'll go and deal with that chicken-faced copper over there, and then I'll come back and sort the old girl out. I won't be a minute.'

'Now, now,' said P.C. Tweedle, dodging behind a chimney. 'I strongly advise you to stand back.'

'Too late for that, mate,' said Jim. 'I'm getting cross now. Come out here!'

'Now, steady on, steady on,' said P.C. Tweedle, darting around one side of the chimney while Jim came round the other. 'What I advise you to do is to count to ten to improve your temper.'

'Keep still!' shouted Jim. 'Stop dodging about like a cuckoo in a clock!'

'I don't want to get my uniform creased, you see –'

'Uniform my foot,' said Jim. 'I know what I can do with you. Come here!'

'No, no, no –'

But when he turned round there was no sign at all of Rose or Miss Gasket. Apart from the constable's legs, the roof was bare.

So he took the suitcase, and clambered back through the skylight, ran down the stairs, and shot out of the Saveloy Hotel like a sirocco.[1] None of the servants knew what hit them.

1. Yes, you guessed it.

CHAPTER EIGHT

'So this was how things stood . . .'
Sergei Sergeievich Prokofiev, *Peter and the Wolf*

SO THIS was how things stood: Lily was caught, and Rose was caught, and Ned was tied up in the dark, and poor little Spangle had been defenestrated. The gangsters had had their cocoa and biscuits and gone to bed early, all except for Filthy, who was still walking around trying to lose his conscience. Mack the Knife had been playing his violin for hours. Every so often he'd stop and sharpen his knife in a meaningful kind of way, and smoke a horrible cigar. Ned wasn't sure which was worst: the cigar, or the knife-sharpening, or the violin-playing – or wondering whether Spangle was all right.

Everything was about as bad as it could be, thought Ned.

He wished the girls would come and bring the locket so that Mack would let him go. If they did, they wouldn't be able to run away properly, though; they'd all have to go begging round the streets, and they'd probably get sent back to the Alderman Cawn-Plaster Memorial Orphanage.

So part of him hoped they wouldn't bring the locket to Mack, but that they'd go and sail away to America as they'd planned, so that at least two of them would be safe and free. He felt very noble when he thought that. He imagined the girls in their prosperous new home in New York or San Francisco, looking sadly at an empty picture-frame draped in black. There'd have been a picture of him if they'd had one, but they didn't, of course, so it would have to be empty. Perhaps they could have little curtains hung across it, and a brass plate saying:

IN MEMORY OF OUR BROTHER NED
WHOSE NOBLE AND FEARLESS NATURE
DID NOT SHRINK FROM THE FINAL SACRIFICE

He thought about that for a good long while, for at least a minute and a half, and decided that there'd probably hardly been anyone as noble as he was, ever. He wished he was a bit more fearless, though. And he wished Spangle would find her way back. She was fearless enough for both of them.

And then once more he heard sharpening sounds from the next room, and the door opened, and there stood Mack . . .

Just then, Ned caught sight of something even more horrible than Mack the Knife.

Crouching up on a high window-ledge, with his eyes glowing and his whiskers bristling and his tail swishing, and with a wisp of sulphurous smoke drifting down from him, sat –

'The devil!' said Ned. 'He's come to get you, look!'

63

Mack laughed. 'No such thing, cocky,' he said. 'And I should know. I'm the most evil man in the world, and I tell you straight, there ain't no devil, there ain't no hell, there ain't no nothing. Except this place, which is bad enough. Now come on – it won't take half a minute.'

'I can see him!' Ned shouted. 'He's up there – his horns, his claws, his tail – he's crouching on the windowsill – he's going to get you! He will, he will!'

'Oh, no, he won't,' said Mack, coming closer.

'Oh, yes, he will!'

'Oh, no, he won't. I know quite well there's nothing on that windowsill, because nothing could climb the warehouse wall. For the last time, there's nothing there!'

That wasn't what Mack had in mind at all.

And as Spring-Heeled Jack came closer and closer, with the hideous glare in his eyes getting fiercer and fiercer, with his whiskers whiskering bristlier and bristlier, Mack sank to his knees.

'Don't take me!' he begged. 'You don't want me – I'm horrible and evil. Take this young lad here – he's got a nice, pure, innocent soul, sweet as a nut!'

'I don't want him,' said Spring-Heeled Jack, coming closer. 'I want you, and I want you now.'

'Oh, blimey,' said Mack faintly. 'Look – what about a bet? Eh?'

'A bet?' said Spring-Heeled Jack, twisting his whiskers. But there was an interested gleam in his eye, and Mack went on:

'Yes! A contest of evil! I'll tell you the most evil thing I can think of, and you tell me the most evil thing you can think of, and we'll see which is the worst. And the one who thinks of that – wins!'

'Hmm,' said Spring-Heeled Jack. 'I like it. I think I'll take you on.'

Mack felt a shudder of relief. He'd thought of so many evil things in his life that he reckoned he was bound to win. He rubbed his hands together – but then Spring-Heeled Jack shook his head.

And off they went, leaving little Ned once more in the dark.

Horrible creepy thoughts crawled all over each other in his mind. He didn't know which would be worse – to be left with Mack, or to be left with the devil. And even if they both vanished, there was still the rest of the gang.

But just as he was feeling completely abandoned, there was an excited little yap in the darkness nearby, and a cold nose snuffled in his neck, and a hot tongue licked eagerly at his cheeks.

'Spangle!' he whispered. 'You're all right! Thank goodness! No – take your tongue out of my nose – stop it – keep quiet – that's a good girl – *ssshh*!'

Spangle was so happy to have found Ned again that she did exactly what he said, even though she couldn't understand it. And as for Ned, he was so happy to have her with him that he felt like licking her. She lay right up close beside him, and they listened as hard as they could.

Then they heard a whispering from next door, like rats' feet pattering over bones. Silence . . . And then a cry of *'Oh no! What a tale of evil! Wicked, wicked!'*

But whose voice was it?

Ned couldn't tell.

And then came more whispering, like the sound of a ghost brushing its long-dead hair in a dusty mirror. Silence. Then –

'No, no, no! I can't bear it! It's too evil for words! I'm done for . . . Horrible, horrible, horrible!'

But whose voice was it?

Ned still couldn't tell. And then there came a lifeless thump as someone fell to the floor . . . And then a slow, dragging noise . . . And then, after a long time, a far distant splash in the river below.

Gulp, thought Ned. Spangle's hair bristled all over, and she gave a tiny howl. She couldn't help it.

Then came a creak as the door opened, and a long shadow fell across the floor . . .

Spring-Heeled Jack

CHAPTER NINE
'AAAAARRGGGHHH!'
David Mostyn, *The Beano*

'**W**ELL?' SAID Ned shakily. 'Who won?'

Slow footsteps came creaking towards him over the dusty floorboards. Spangle's nose was trembling in his neck, and his eyes were shut tight, and there was a horrible silence.

Then Ned felt hands on his shoulders, lifting him gently up.

'Well done, Ned,' said the voice of the devil.

Ned felt him undoing the rope, and opened his eyes. And then he saw that it couldn't have been the devil, because Spangle was licking him furiously, so he must have been all right.

Pausing only to tie the other gangsters (who were fast asleep) firmly into their beds so they wouldn't be able to get out till the police came, Jack and Ned and Spangle went down the rickety old stairs and out on to the dark wharf.

WE'LL ROW UP THE RIVER – IT'S THE QUICKEST WAY TO BLACKFRIARS.

But while Jack was untying a convenient rowing-boat . . .

Whatever it was that Spring-Heeled Jack had told him, it hadn't been enough to finish Mack off. His leathery old soul had been scorched a bit, but the water must have cooled him down, because he came crawling out as evil as ever and thirsting for revenge.

And he nearly had it, too.

But Spangle saved the day. She made straight for him as if she'd been shot from a catapult. Her little teeth were snapping, and her little paws were scratching, and the growl that came out of her throat would have done credit to a werewolf.

'So you didn't need me after all?' said Spring-Heeled Jack, when Ned and Spangle had finished. 'Just sit on him for a minute and we'll tie him up.'

And taking a rope from the boat, he leapt into the air on his spring-heeled boots and passed the end through a pulley at the very top of the warehouse.

'He can stay there till the police come and take him down,' said Jack, as they rowed up the river. 'It's a nice view from up there. He'll enjoy it if he stops wriggling.'

CHAPTER TEN

'You mustn't cry, my dear . . .'
Russell Hoban, *The Mouse and His Child*

POLLY WAS ever so miserable. She was so unhappy that the landlord of the Rose and Crown stopped her serving in the bar and made her go and do the washing-up instead. Tears in the dishwater didn't matter, but tears in the beer made it taste funny, and the customers complained.

She was longing for Jim to come back so she could have a really good howl. But he wasn't due back for about two years, and thinking of that made her cry even more, and she had to empty the tears out of the bowl and put some fresh water in.

So when she looked up and saw Jim's face at the scullery window, she gave a yelp of surprise.

He told Polly what had happened, and they sat down by the kitchen fire, feeling miserable.

'I reckon we've let 'em both down, Polly,' said Jim. 'Poor little kids. D'you know what?'

'What?'

'I don't reckon they ought to get away with it, them Superintendents. I reckon someone ought to put a stop to it.'

'But you ought to be getting back to your ship, Jim! And you got that gentleman's suitcase to take, and all . . .'

'I don't care about that, Poll. This is a matter of a sailor's honour!'

He looked so noble sitting there, with his fists on his knees and his jaw clenched, that he might have been the sailor William in the play *Black-Ey'd Susan*, about to be hanged from the yardarm.

'Oh, Jim,' she said.

And she might easily have kissed him or something, except that he suddenly stopped looking noble and looked excited instead.

'Here, Poll,' he said, 'I've just had a brainwave! Supposing them guardians thought the kids' Ma and Pa had turned up – they'd have to let 'em go, wouldn't they?'

— BRAINWAVE

81

'Well, I suppose they would, Jim, but – what are you doing?'

Jim had flung open the suitcase and was rummaging around among the clothes. He found a suit and held it up against himself.

'There,' he said. 'We could pretend to be them, couldn't we? How's that?'

Polly didn't know what to say. So she dried her eyes and kissed him.

'Oh, Jim!' she said, having found some words. 'All right, we'll do it!'

So they disguised themselves, and set out for the Alderman Cawn-Plaster Memorial Orphanage.

And only a minute or two later by the kitchen clock, the cat suddenly sat up.

Spring-Heeled Jack usually came to the scullery door when he visited Polly, because if he'd come in through the front door, none of the customers would ever have gone there again.

But Polly wasn't there, and nor were the girls. Ned was so tired that he sat down with Spangle and went to sleep, while Spring-Heeled Jack crept through the whole house and found no one.

Something was wrong. It wasn't like Polly to vanish like that. Jack went back to the kitchen, where Ned was nearly fast asleep, and there he spotted the suitcase.

Spring-Heeled Jack

CHAPTER ELEVEN

'Meanwhile, back at the orphanage . . .'
Philip Pullman, *Spring-Heeled Jack*

MEANWHILE, BACK at the orphanage, Mr Killjoy and Miss Gasket were congratulating themselves.

They sat in Mr Killjoy's office eating cheese-and-pickle sandwiches and drinking sarsaparilla cordial. Mr Killjoy put some brandy in his, because he found it helped his digestion.

He was just about to look at it when there was a ring at the doorbell.

Mr Killjoy jumped, and stuffed the locket into his waistcoat.

'Who can that be?' he whispered.

'Oh, bless my soul, it's the police – it's that man that got stuffed down the chimney –'

'Not your responsibility, Miss Gasket – deny everything!'

The bell rang again, louder.

'Come on, open up!' came a voice from outside. 'We know you're in there!'

'Better go and let them in, Miss Gasket,' said Mr Killjoy hurriedly.

She scuttled out. He took a quick swig of brandy and made sure the account-books were out of sight, just in case the visitors should be troubled by trying to work out what some of the entries meant.

A moment later, Miss Gasket showed Jim and Polly in.

Polly had rouged and powdered her face, and she was wearing a very grand dress that the landlord's missus had worn to the Gas-Fitters' Ball. She hadn't told the landlord's missus, and there'd be ructions later, but this was an emergency. Jim was wearing one of Mr Summers' suits. He'd stuck on a great big false pair of whiskers as well, but he wasn't at all sure of them.

Mr Killjoy began to swell up and go red, so Polly thought she'd better step in.

'Please, sir,' she said, 'you'll have to forgive me dear husband, him having gone through torments in the Australian goldfields, 'cause he's a bit upset, as I am meself. You see, we've heard that our dear little children, what we believed was lost, is in your care!'

'We'll have to see about that,' said Miss Gasket tightly.

'Too right you will,' said Jim.

'Now, now, dear,' said Polly. Then she announced: 'Our names is Mr and Mrs Summers, and our kiddies' names is Lily, Rose and Ned.'

Well, that took Mr Killjoy by surprise.

She had a gleam in her eye. To Mr Killjoy's astonishment, she turned back to Polly and said, 'Very well, Mrs Summers, dear. You shall have them.'

She left the room. They all watched her go, and then turned back to each other.

There was a very awkward silence indeed. Jim was looking suspiciously at Mr Killjoy, and Mr Killjoy was looking suspiciously at Jim, and Polly was trying to look innocent.

'Very seasonable weather we're having,' she said brightly.

No one said a word.

'Very seasonable for the time of year, I mean,' she said.

And then the door opened, and there was a double gasp.

Miss Gasket seemed to be enjoying herself, and nobody could work out why. Then she sprang a surprise.

'Before we can release the dear little ones into your care,' she said sweetly, 'there's the Orphanage Regulations to be complied with.'

'Oh, yes?' said Jim. 'I don't see any need for that.'

'Just a little check,' said Miss Gasket, 'to make sure no one's impersonating anyone they ain't.'

Polly gulped. But there was no way round that, and she and Jim had to take the pieces of paper and the pencils Miss Gasket handed out. She gave some to Rose and Lily too, and they all waited nervously for what Miss Gasket would say next.

'Now then,' she said. 'It's very simple. You can all write down the answers to three questions. And if your answers match up with the girls' ones, why, you can take them away!'

'It's no good, sweetheart,' Jim whispered, 'I reckon we'll just have to give way to despair!'

'Question number one,' said Miss Gasket, smiling like a crocodile. 'What was the name of the little cottage where you all lived before you was so sadly split up?'

'Oh! Oh!' said Polly. 'I think I'm going to faint!'

And she pressed the back of her hand to her head and sank to the floor with a graceful thump.

As soon as he'd written it down, he rushed over to Polly. But he knew she was only pretending, and it had given him an idea about what to do next.

'There, there, me love,' he said. 'All right now?'

'Oh, I don't know what came over me,' said Polly, heaving herself delicately up. 'There, I'm quite restored.'

'Oh, good,' said Miss Gasket. 'And now for the second question: what's the date of Lily's birthday?'

That was a tricky one. But it only took Jim a second to think of a way round it.

So far so good. Polly scribbled the answer down, and then rushed to the window with the others.

'Where? Where is it?' she said.

'It's gone now,' said Jim. 'You missed it. What a shame.'

They all stood away from the window. Mr Killjoy had got a bit bumped in the rush, mainly by Jim, and he wasn't very happy about it.

But Miss Gasket was impatient to get on. Jim was wondering what Polly would think of this time, and wondering whether he ought to think of something in case she couldn't, and wondering how they'd manage if neither of them did; but mainly, he was bothered by a stray bit of whisker that was sticking up his nose.

'And now we come to the third question,' said Miss Gasket. 'What was –'

But finally he realized.

'Oh, that's the end, then,' he said bitterly. 'But I tell you this – I think it's a blooming disgrace!'

'That's the first true thing you've said tonight, young man,' said Mr Killjoy. 'Miss Gasket, go and fetch Sergeant Pincher from the police station!'

'With the greatest of pleasure,' said Miss Gasket, and she went out into the hall to put on her galoshes, her fox-fur tippet, and her hat with the left-hand half of a tropical bird stuck to it.

She was too stingy to take a candle with her, and she knew where everything was without looking, or so she thought. So she had the shock of her life when she reached for the door handle and found – a hand!

It was a hard, cold hand, and it gripped hers with iron strength. You should have heard her scream! It made plaster fall from the ceiling (what little there was of it) and it woke all the children in the orphanage.

They came crowding out of their cold beds and peered down the chilly stairs, and the sight that met their eyes was enough to curdle water.

For there in the light of the lamp held in Mr Killjoy's horrified hand, as he opened the door of the office, was –

THE DEVIL !

UNHAND ME, MEPHISTOPHELES !

NO, DON'T. CARRY ON HANDING HER !

THE DEVIL'S COME FOR MISS GASKET !

TAKE HER ALL THE WAY DOWN !

HE'S GOT HER AT LAST –

GOOD FOR MISTER POTOFLEAS !

HOORAY !

HOORAY !

As for Mr Killjoy, he couldn't believe his eyes. He'd had either too much brandy or too little, and he couldn't decide which.

But then the frightful vision spoke, in tones of thunder.

'I am Spring-Heeled Jack,' he said. 'And I want to have words with you.'

And in came Spangle like a rocket. She knew Spring-Heeled Jack now, so she didn't waste any sniffs on him, but there were enough strange smells in the orphanage to keep her happy for hours. She didn't fancy Mr Killjoy's smell very much, so she just gave his ankle a nip and then bounded up the stairs to smell all the kids. They were delighted.

Mr Killjoy and Miss Gasket could tell they weren't wanted down there, and they were about to sneak upstairs and beat a few of the children to relieve their feelings, when Spring-Heeled Jack put out a claw-like hand and stopped them.

And Mr Killjoy went scuttling into the office after them to make certain Mr Hawkshaw heard about some of the things Miss Gasket had done wrong.

'Spring-Heeled Jack?' said Rose. 'What's going to happen to us now? Can we get on that ship and go to America?'

'Yes,' he said. 'And, in fact, I've got a surprise for you. But we'll have to hurry. Ned! Lily!'

But Rose had something important to say first.

'Please,' she said, plucking at his sleeve. 'It's all the others. It don't seem fair somehow, but I know they can't all come with us, only I would like 'em to be a bit better off than what they are . . .'

Spring-Heeled Jack looked up the dark stairs. The landing was crowded with faces, silent and wide-eyed in the gloom.

And among them was Spangle. She was as quiet as all the rest, and every so often looked up and licked the nearest dirty face. Ned could tell what she wanted from the way she was looking at him, and he could tell what all the kids wanted, too.

So he said, 'Spring-Heeled Jack? You know Spangle? Well, she – well, I mean – could you – I mean, they don't let 'em have pets here, but maybe – and she'd probably fall off the ship anyway – and – could they keep her here?'

Leaving Spangle was even more difficult than facing up to Mack the Knife. But after all, he and Rose and Lily were going to be free now, and none of the others were. And Spangle would certainly look after them well.

'I understand,' said Spring-Heeled Jack. 'Well, I don't think Mr Killjoy or Miss Gasket will be here for very long, and there's bound to be a change in the rules about pets and things. The new Superintendent will see to that.'

'Who's that going to be?' said Rose.

'And what's going to happen to Polly?' said Lily. 'She'll lose her job when the landlord's missus finds out about the dress . . .'

'If you put two and two together,' said Spring-Heeled Jack, 'you'll come up with the answer. Leave it all to me. And now we must hurry. We've got to get to the Docks before Jim's ship sails.'

'Oh, yes,' said Jim. 'That gentleman'll be wanting his suitcase.'

'It's more important than that,' said Spring-Heeled Jack. 'That gentleman is – the children's father!'

SENSATION CONT: PAGE 103

GOOD, ISN'T IT– EH?

'Yes,' said Spring-Heeled Jack, 'the name on the suitcase is Edward Montgomery Summers, and if he isn't your father, I'm a cucumber. Come on – I've got a cab waiting – but we'll have to be quick!'

Ned shot up the stairs and said goodbye to Spangle, and the girls said goodbye to Polly and all the kids.

'Oh – quick –' said Rose, fumbling for the locket. 'We won't need this now – I'll take the picture out – and then can you sell it and give the money to the orphanage so the kids can have some decent blankets?'

'Yes,' said Spring-Heeled Jack. 'But *hurry.*'

There was just time for a tender farewell.

CHAPTER TWELVE

'We haven't a moment to lose, Captain . . .'
Hergé, *The Adventures of Tintin: The Shooting Star*

They hadn't a moment to lose. The terrified cab-driver hung on with both hands as Spring-Heeled Jack took the reins and cracked the whip and set the horse galloping through the empty streets towards the Docks, with the children holding tight inside and Jim (and the suitcase) clinging on behind.

Already the sky was lighter in the east, and the tide was plucking and knocking at the ships in the dock. The Captain was about to give orders for the gangplank to be raised. A fat little tug was puffing and snorting nearby.

In his cabin, Mr Summers was fast asleep, dreaming of his lost children. Into his sleep came the distant sounds of the sailors reefing the binnacle and close-hauling the anchor chain, and the distant smells of breakfast from the galley.

'Not long now,' he murmured.

The sailors on the tug threw a stout rope up to the sailors on the *Indomitable*, and they tied it tightly to a solid bit of ship. The Captain watched to make sure they didn't use a granny knot.

Meanwhile, Spring-Heeled Jack was driving like a demon. The cab was hurtling through the streets, swaying round corners, rattling over cobblestones, and shaking the children about like nobody's business.

They'd just lurched around a corner into the West India Dock Road when –

Spread out all over the road were a ton and a half of Brussels sprouts. A wagon belonging to the Amalgamated East Anglian Brussels Sprout Company had overturned on its way to the market, and a heap of the little vegetables spread from one side of the road to the other.

And leaving the cab-driver thanking his lucky stars that they'd finished with his cab, they set off on foot, running as they'd never run before.

The ship's hooter sounded one long blast over the rooftops.

'Oh, no –' gasped Lily. 'We'll never make it –'

'RUN!' said Spring-Heeled Jack.

On the ship, Mr Summers had got dressed and come out on deck to watch as they left the shores of England behind.

The tug had brought the sharp end of the ship round to face the right way. The dock gates were open; the tide was at its height. Mr Summers stood at the blunt end, leaning on the rail, looking back over the warehouses and the cranes and the rooftops as the ship moved slowly out of the dock.

Suddenly he stood up straight and rubbed his eyes. Leaping over the dock wall came a strange, devilish figure – and then, running in past the Customs shed, came a sailor with a suitcase, and one – two – three children . . .

The sailors on the tug avasted, and the tug stopped tugging.

And a minute or two later, the children were in the jolly-boat, and so was Jim, and so was the suitcase.

And a minute or two after that . . .

But Spring-Heeled Jack had vanished.

The tide couldn't wait any longer. The sailors made fast the capstans and broached the hawsers, and the ship moved out into the busy river.

But we haven't quite finished with the streets yet.

Just at the very fag-end of the night, a little wispy creature, hardly visible, hardly there at all, could have been seen (with a little imagination) pulling at the sleeve of a certain weary villain.

COME ON! NOT FAR NOW!

DON'T YOU EVER GIVE UP?

JUST ONE MORE CORNER.

And around that corner –

Just then, who should come round the corner but the pieman.

And out on the ocean blue, the good ship *Indomitable* was steaming for the New World.

Read on for a preview of

COUNT KARLSTEIN

ONE

PETER CROUCHED over the fire, stirring the embers so that the sparks swarmed up like imps on the rocky walls of hell. Behind him, his shadow shook and flared across the wall and half the ceiling of our little bedroom, and the cracks between the floorboards shone like golden rivers in the darkness.

'Listen,' he said. 'Zamiel!'

And with a delicious shiver I pulled my eiderdown over me and lay on the rug with my face pressed to the floor to hear the voices from the parlour below . . .

We lived in the tavern in Karlstein village, with our ma, who was the landlady. A quiet enough place, though there was usually a stranger or two passing through, and the company in the tavern parlour was as good as any in the mountains – especially on a winter's night, when their pipes were going and their glasses full and there was a good story to be told.

Peter and I each had our favourites: stories of hunting for him and tales of terror for me. The best of all were those about Zamiel, the Prince of the Mountains, the Demon Huntsman. There was usually a bargain in the tale, and a chase, and bloody revenge, and a frenzied victim running in terror through the snow, pursued by the Wild Hunt – great hounds with slavering jaws and luminous eyes, black horses ridden by grinning skeletons and, at the head of it all, the Demon himself, swathed in impenetrable darkness, with eyes of raging fire. Even our ma (we'd see through the cracks in the floorboards) would pause in her work and lean her plump elbows on the counter and stare with wide eyes as the latest tale unfolded.

But none of the customers below ever came so close to Zamiel as Peter and I did, and I came closest of all: I was in the very room when he came for his victim, and I'll never forget what I saw if I live till the year 1900.

It all began on a grey afternoon in October. The year was 1816, and I'd been working at Castle Karlstein for nearly a year. (My name is Hildi, by the way.) There had been a heavy fall of snow; I was sitting at the parlour window with a bundle of mending in my lap, and Miss Lucy and Miss Charlotte behind me were roasting chestnuts in the fire. I was looking out at the fading light and thinking of drawing the curtains to shut out the chill when I saw a coach lumbering up the narrow road. I gazed at it in surprise, because we'd had no visitors since March; and then, as the coach turned the corner into the castle courtyard, the wheels slipped on the icy road and the coach slewed round towards the precipice.

The horses whinnied with fear and the driver nearly fell off the box as the brakes screeched and failed to grip; the coach banged against the stone gateway, and came away lighter by a great strip of paint. I jumped and cried out – and then at the last moment the wheels gripped, and the coach rolled through into the courtyard. The girls ran up beside me and watched as the coachman got down and leaned shivering against the large back wheel, and mopped his forehead before opening the door of the coach.

Out there stepped, cool as you please, a skinny old gentleman in black, who looked at the coachman as if to say, 'Nerves? I advise you to have 'em cut out, my man, and braided into a whip, the better to guide these shambling nags,' dusted off the flakes of snow that had had the impertinence to settle on his bony old shoulders, and made his way across the white courtyard, where the darkness was already beginning to pile up in the corners, as if driven there by the wind. Johann the footman opened the castle door and let out a great quantity of light, which leapt inside again as soon as he shut it. The coachman began to unharness the horses, with many head-shakings and gesturings to the groom, while the girls tried to guess who the visitor might be.

They were English – not Swiss at all, though they'd picked up enough of our language in the time they'd been here to sound like natives. Lucy was twelve and Charlotte was ten, and I wasn't much older myself; but I counted myself more fortunate by far, because I had a mother still alive and a brother – and no grim uncle like Count Karlstein. They had no other relatives, and since their parents had both died in a shipwreck, they had no choice but Count Karlstein or an orphanage – and if they'd known what he'd be like, they'd have chosen the orphanage without a second's pause. They'd been here a year now, poor things.

He'd been here for nine, nearly. Old Count Ludwig Karlstein, the previous count, had died without an heir, so the estate had passed to Count Heinrich Karlstein, a thin, dark man, much given to gnawing his nails, muttering to himself, and poring over works of German philosophy at midnight in his stone-walled, tapestried study. Nothing so bad in those things, of course, but he had other defects, such as a temper you'd have put down for its own sake if it'd been a dog, a vile, sarcastic tongue, and – worst of all – a kind of bright-eyed delight in being cruel, whether it was to a horse or dog or a servant – or a little niece from another country, with nowhere else to go. But there it was: he was the master.

And meanwhile, Lucy had remembered who the visitor was.

'It's the lawyer, Charlotte!' she insisted. 'The old man from Geneva! He gave us that dark sweet wine and some cake while we waited for Uncle Heinrich—'

'Meister Haifisch!' said Charlotte.

'That's right. Perhaps he's come to take us away again – can he do that? D'you think he could do that, Hildi?'

'Hildi, go and find out! Go and listen! Please!' said Charlotte.

'I can't do that!' I said. 'They'd throw me out for good, and then where would you be? Just wait and see, that's the best thing to do.'

Lucy made a face, but she saw I was right. And as it happened, none of us had long to wait, because only a minute or so later Frau Muller the housekeeper (as surly as a goose, and with the same way of leaning at you with a long neck when she was cross) came bustling in.

'Miss Lucy and Miss Charlotte! You're to go and wash yourselves and brush your hair and come down to your Uncle Heinrich in ten minutes. And you, Kelmar, put that sewing down and get along to the drawing-room – Dettweiler fell over in the courtyard and broke her ankle, stupid girl, so you'll have to be parlourmaid for the time being.'

They were hustled away, and I took a candle and hastened down to the drawing-room. Poor little Susi Dettweiler – Count Karlstein had made her cry three times yesterday, and now she breaks her ankle! My heart was thumping wildly as I went in, in case my clumsiness attracted Count Karlstein's attention. I feared he'd lash at me like a tiger.

But when I opened the door, I saw him so deep in conversation with the skinny old stranger, and the skinny old stranger paying such close attention to him, that neither of them noticed me for a moment or two. I don't know what I should have done, but I stood in the shadows, too nervous to go forward, and listened to what they were saying.

'Damn it, Haifisch,' said Count Karlstein (Haifisch! Lucy was right, then: this cool old skeleton was the lawyer from Geneva), 'you're not *sure*? After nine years? How much longer d'you want? Would a hundred years be sufficient? Would you be able to say then, "Yes, Count Karlstein, we have finally established that there is no other claimant – for if there was, he must be dead by now"? Eh?'

Meister Haifisch showed no sign that Count Karlstein's tone annoyed him. He was as calm as he'd been when he'd stepped out of the coach, having missed certain death by the thickness of a wheel rim.

'You asked me to make certain, Count Karlstein,' he said evenly. 'Certainty without evidence, in a case like this, is worthless.'

Count Karlstein snorted. 'Worthless! *You're* worthless, Haifisch, if you can't do better than that. If evidence is all you want, can't you manufacture some? Eh? Make it up?'

The lawyer stood up. That was all he did; but it stopped Count Karlstein's restless prowling and finger-gnawing and sideways kicks at the great log in the fire as effectively as if a gunshot had sounded. Meister

Haifisch had a presence that commanded your attention. Like an actor, he knew how to make every movement count. And his audience – both of us, one in the shadows beside the door and one scowling beside the fire – was held still, waiting for his next words.

Which were simple. 'Good night, Count Karlstein,' was all he said; but his voice held such a charge of contempt that it would have shamed the devil himself.

'Oh, sit down, man,' said Count Karlstein irritably; and I knew he'd realized that if he wanted to tamper with the truth, Meister Haifisch wasn't the man to put a legal seal on the doing of it. 'Come and sit down again. I'm out of sorts – don't mind me. Go through it again, will ye . . . ?' And he threw himself into the carved oak chair at the other side of the fireplace, bent down to tear off a strip of bark from one of the logs in the hearth, and shredded it slowly into tiny pieces as Meister Haifisch spoke.

'The only son of old Count Ludwig Karlstein was stolen from his cradle twenty years ago. I have traced him as far as Geneva, where a child answering to the same description was placed in a foundlings' home a short while after he disappeared. That child – if it was he – grew up and became a groom, working in the stables of the Black Bear Inn; then he joined the army – and that is the last we know. His regiment was scattered at the Battle of Bodelheim; he may have been taken prisoner, or he may be dead. And that, I repeat, is all we know.'

Count Karlstein grunted and slapped his thigh in irritation.

'That's the best you can do?'

'That is the best anyone can do, Count Karlstein. There is no one in Switzerland who knows more about the affairs of the estate of Karlstein than I do; and so what I have told is the limit of human knowledge on the subject.'

Was there a hint of sarcasm in his tone? Maybe, but Count Karlstein didn't hear it if there was. For he looked up then, and saw me. He sprang to his feet with an oath.

'How long have you been there, hussy?' he snarled.

'Only a moment, sir! I knocked, but you didn't hear me!'

The lawyer was watching; otherwise I think the count would have hit me. He sent me out impatiently to fetch some wine, and when I came back, I found that he and Meister Haifisch had given up all attempts at conversation and were standing at opposite ends of the room, examining the books, or the pictures, or the snow-filled darkness outside the window.

I served them the wine, and then the girls came in; Meister Haifisch bent and shook their hands, and asked them how they were; and a warmth came into his expression. He looked as dry as dust and no more kindly than a silver ink-pot, but he was as polite and attentive to those two little girls as if they'd been the Duchess of Savoy and her twin sister. Lucy and Charlotte blossomed, and sat on the sofa at either side of him, sipping their wine and talking with all the elegance in the world, while their uncle prowled, gnawing his fingers, around the edges of the room and said nothing.

Presently Meister Haifisch stood up and bowed to the girls, excusing himself, as it was time to dress for dinner; and while I cleared away the glasses, Count Karlstein came and stood by the fire again and said to them:

'Lucy, Charlotte – how long have you been here now? A year, is it?'

'Almost, Uncle Heinrich,' said Lucy.

The count looked down. Then abruptly he said, 'How would you like a holiday?'

Both the girls looked startled for a moment, then nodded vigorously.

'We'd love it,' said Lucy.

'Leaving tomorrow afternoon,' he said, beaming, trying to be genial. 'Just a few days, mind.'

'Anything!' said Charlotte, eagerly.

'Where would we be going?' said Lucy.

'To my hunting lodge,' said Count Karlstein.

Their faces dropped involuntarily – but only for a second, and then they recovered. He didn't notice.

'That would be very pleasant, Uncle Heinrich,' said Lucy.

'Thank you very much,' said Charlotte, trying as hard as she could to keep the disappointment out of her voice.

'Good, good, that's settled then,' said the count, and dismissed them briskly, settling down at his desk and scribbling at some papers. I followed the girls out.

They were neither of them keen on hunting; and if you don't like hunting, where's the fun in staying at a hunting lodge? Deep in the middle of the forest, all set about with pine trees . . . Set about with wolves, too, and bears and wild boars. What would the girls do there but struggle through the deep snow and watch Count Karlstein hack the life out of some poor deer his bullets had brought twitching to the ground? What would they do in the evening but sit wrapped in furs beside the skimpy fire and watch Count Karlstein getting drunk with his chief huntsman? A fine holiday they'd have!

And then I realized something that brought a little chill to my heart. Today was Wednesday; they were leaving tomorrow, Thursday, and staying, said the count, for a few days . . . which meant that they'd be at the hunting lodge on All Souls' Eve, Friday night – the very night when Zamiel the Demon Huntsman was said to ride through the forests, driving every living thing before him. Scorched hoofprints were found after his passing, they said, and animals dead of terror, with no mark upon them . . .

But I couldn't tell Charlotte and Lucy that. There're things best kept quiet, for fear of making them worse. So I said nothing – for the moment.

ABOUT THE AUTHOR

PHILIP PULLMAN was born in 1946 in Norwich, Norfolk. He spent a lot of his childhood on board ships, as his father and stepfather were both in the Royal Air Force and his mother and brother seemed to be constantly following them around the world by sea.

Philip read English at Oxford University and for a long time he taught in schools before becoming a full-time writer. He is now one of our best storytellers. He has written many books for children and has won numerous awards for his work.

The Firework-Maker's Daughter was a Gold Medal Smarties prize-winner, *Clockwork* was a Silver Medal Smarties prize-winner, and *Northern Lights*, the first volume in his trilogy, *His Dark Materials*, won the Carnegie Medal and was joint winner of the Guardian

Children's Fiction Prize. His novel *The Amber Spyglass* was the first ever children's book to win the overall Whitbread Award. The *His Dark Materials* trilogy has been made into an acclaimed production at the National Theatre. Philip Pullman lives in Oxford, and is married with two sons.

CLOCKWORK

Tick, tick, tick, tock. **Once you've wound some things up, nothing can stop them . . .**

It is a cold winter's night when Karl enters the White Horse Tavern looking like he's swallowed a thundercloud. His final task as a clockmaker apprentice is to make a new figure for the great clock of Glockenheim. He has not made the figure – or got any idea of what it could be, and the unveiling is tomorrow.

Fritz is also in the tavern; there to read aloud his new spooky story. Like Karl, he hasn't finished. Well, he knows how the story starts and he knows it's called *Clockwork* – so, with the snow swirling down outside, he sets his story going and just has to hope that the ending will come to him as he tells it.

Suddenly, Fritz's story and real life merge in a completely sinister way – and just like clockwork it can't be stopped . . .

'Exciting, scary, romantic and deliciously readable'
Guardian

'Makes the hair stand up on the back of your neck'
Jacqueline Wilson

I WAS A RAT!

**A fairy tale filled with fun and magic for
young and old from the master storyteller
and creator of *His Dark Materials***

'*I was a rat!*' Roger insists, and insists . . . In fact,
when Bob the cobbler and his washerwoman wife,
Joan, find the young boy abandoned on their
doorstep, these are the only words he says.
And he does have ratty behaviour, it's true.

Staying with Bob and Joan, however, Roger learns
quickly to behave more like a human child. They try
to find his parents, but the orphanage, police and
hospital all have nothing on their records about a lost
boy in the city. What is the truth? As more and more
people find out about Roger the mysterious rat-boy he
faces more and more danger. But sometimes help
comes from the most unexpected of places . . .

'Fairy tale, satire, slapstick humour and suspenseful
melodrama . . . a glorious tale' *Guardian*

'A comic genius of children's fiction' *The Times*

THE SCARECROW AND HIS SERVANT

To tell the truth, Jack felt a little nervous, because it isn't every day you find a scarecrow talking to you . . .

One night, during a terrible thunderstorm, a boy named Jack shelters in a barn. The following morning he is confused to find a scarecrow with a turnip head calling out to him. For a moment he thinks he is imagining it. But he isn't – the scarecrow has been struck by lightning in exactly the right way to bring him completely to life.

Jack becomes the scarecrow's personal servant, and together they decide to set out and see the world. It is a journey that neither of them could have possibly imagined, filled with adventure – and it will change them both in ways they never expected . . .

'A perfectly made gem, full of fun, fireworks and wit. We continue to be lucky to have Pullman writing for us' *Guardian*